STORIES
to Learn By

STORIES to Learn By

Revised Edition

Written by
Monsignor John H. Koenig

Illustrated by
Christine Huddleston

*P*auline
BOOKS & MEDIA
BOSTON

Library of Congress Cataloging-in-Publication Data

Koenig, John H.
    Stories to learn by / written by Monsignor John H. Koenig; illustrated by Christine Huddleston.—Rev. ed.
        p.   cm.
    Summary: A collection of twelve stories in which characters experience the value of Christian living.
    ISBN 0-8198-6993-7 (pbk.)
    1. Christian life Juvenile fiction.   2. Children's stories, American.   [1. Christian life Fiction. 2. Short stories.]   I. Huddleston, Christine, ill.   II. Title.
PZ7.K81797St   1999
[Fic]—dc21   99-23030
                                                                                                          CIP

Printed and published in the U.S.A. by Pauline Books & Media, 50 Saint Pauls Avenue, Boston, MA 02130-3491.

www.pauline.org

Pauline Books & Media is the publishing house of the Daughters of St. Paul, an international congregation of women religious serving the Church with the communications media.

1 2 3 4 5 6   05   04 03 02 01 00

Contents

A Note to Parents and Teachers

Stories to Learn By is designed to provide hours of enjoyable and entertaining reading, while at the same time introducing fundamental human and Christian values to young children.

Before beginning to read this collection with your child or children, it would be best to explain that these are all "make-believe" stories which did not really happen. You might also like to point out that although they are only "make-believe," they can teach us many good and important things.

B. Benny Bumpkin

Once there was a baby boy named Bartholomew Benjamin Bumpkin.

Now that's quite a long name for a tiny baby, isn't it? So everyone called him B. Benny for short.

B. Benny was such a happy baby! His mom and dad loved him. So did everyone else.

B. Benny grew and grew as all babies do. He grew so big and so strong that soon he could sit right up straight in a highchair. One sunny day he even learned to walk. Or at least he took three steps all by himself, and, as everyone knows, that's the way to begin walking.

B. Benny learned to eat all by himself and only spill a tiny bit. Next he started to talk. And little by little he even learned to read.

Bartholomew Benjamin Bumpkin did have one small problem, though. Every so often, and there was no telling when, he would topple over backward. Floors are not very soft, and with all his tumbles B. Benny soon became a very bumped-up Bumpkin. And so his mother had to tie a pillow behind him. From then on, wherever B. Benny went the pillow was sure to follow.

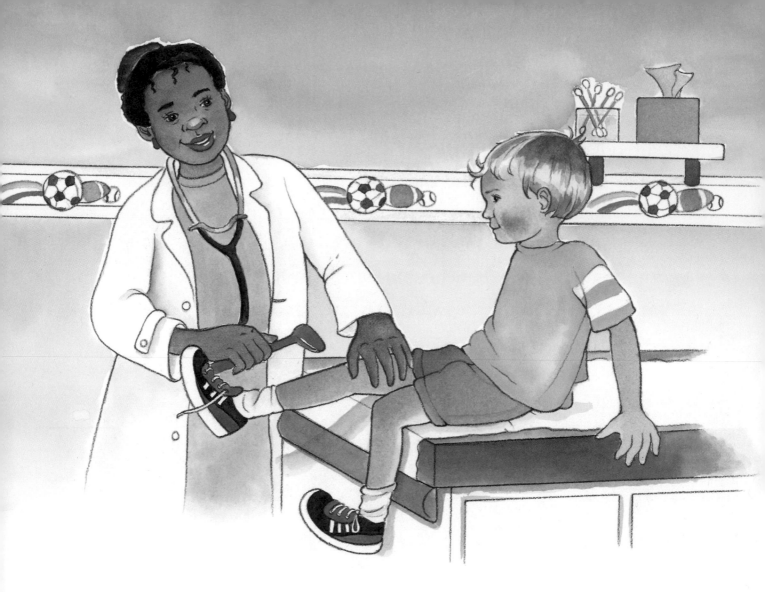

His mother, of course, was worried about Benny's tumbles. She brought him to the doctor for a check-up. The doctor carefully examined B. Benny, but she really couldn't find anything wrong with him. Benny had strong legs and strong ankles. He had good clear eyes and everything a healthy little boy should have. Benny even had a smile that played all over his face.

The doctor asked some questions.

"Does he eat his cereal in the morning?"

"Yes, he does, Doctor," said his mother.

"Does he get plenty of exercise?"

"Yes," nodded his mother.

"Does he eat all the vegetables on his plate?"

"Oh, yes!" his mother said once again.

"How about his vitamins? Does he take them when he should?"

"Yes, he never skips them," his mother said proudly.

The doctor took Benny's temperature. She even put him on a scale and weighed him. But everything was fine.

Finally the doctor said, "I can't find anything wrong with B. Benny, Mrs. Bumpkin."

And so his mother took him home. But the very next day, B. Benny toppled over backward again. His mother picked up the phone and called the doctor. "What should I do?" she asked in a worried voice.

"I really can't say," answered the doctor, "but for now, get a bigger pillow!"

And so it was that B. Benny became known for miles around as the little boy who always wore a pillow.

B. Benny continued to grow...and to fall, too. One summer his mother and father sent B. Benny to camp for a vacation. Of course he brought along his pillow.

B. Benny shared a cabin with a boy named Peter. Now that first night at camp, when the bugle blew for everyone to put out their lights and go to sleep, B. Benny did what he always did. He slipped off the pillow he was wearing and slid into bed.

But not Peter! Peter got down on his knees beside his bed. He blessed himself and began to say his prayers.

"What are you doing?" asked B. Benny, who was watching.

Peter looked a little surprised. "I'm praying," he said.

"Praying?" asked B. Benny. "What's that?"

"It's talking to God," Peter explained.

B. Benny looked confused, so Peter explained some more. "God is our Father in heaven. God made you and me and all people. God made the world and everything in it—all the animals and plants, the sun, moon and stars, the oceans—just every-thing you can think of!"

Benny's eyes got very wide. *Wow!* he thought to himself.

"Every night I thank God for all the great things he's done," Peter told Benny. "I also ask God for things I need and for things other people need," Peter said. "And then I ask God to forgive me for any wrong things I've done. I ask him to help me to do better next time."

B. Benny thought about all this for a minute. "Would God listen to me, too, Peter?" he asked.

"You bet!" Peter grinned. "Want to try talking to him?"

Benny nodded and bounced out of bed. He knelt down beside Peter. "I'll teach you a very special prayer, Benny, the one that Jesus taught us," Peter said. Benny repeated each word after Peter: "Our Father who art in heaven, hallowed be thy name; thy kingdom come; thy will be done on earth as it is in heaven. Give us this day our daily bread; and forgive us our trespasses as we forgive those who trespass against us; and lead us not into temptation, but deliver us from evil. Amen." When they finished praying the Our Father, B. Benny climbed back into bed. He felt very happy. He had a

good mother and father on earth and now he knew he also had a good Father in heaven. Best of all B. Benny had started talking to God!

But that was only the beginning. Before they fell asleep that night, Peter told Benny all about God's wonderful love for us. He told Benny that God is always with us and is always ready to listen to us. Peter explained that we can pray to God in our own words, too. God loves every prayer we say.

B. Benny was very happy to learn all this! He started talking to God more and more.

The next day came and went and B. Benny only fell twice. That night he knelt down with Peter and they prayed together again. The following day came and went with not even one topple or tumble. And so it went day by day with only a topple here and there until B. Benny's vacation was over and it was time to go home.

On his first day back home B. Benny only had one tiny tumble. His mother couldn't believe her eyes! Another tiny topple came on the third day, but by then Benny didn't need to wear his pillow anymore.

Now Bartholomew Benjamin Bumpkin hardly ever tumbles or topples. And the secret is really quite simple. B. Benny needed exercise and good, wholesome food. He needed to learn to walk and talk and read and count. But most of all, Benny needed to learn about his loving Father in heaven. And he needed to learn how to pray. To this very day B. Benny Bumpkin never has to wear a pillow and to this very day B. Benny never forgets to pray!

Kim Becomes Brave

Mommy, I don't want an operation! I just don't want it!"
Kim tugged at her mother's coat. Big tears rolled down her cheeks.
Kim and her mother had just come from the doctor's office. The

20

doctor had said that Kim's tonsils were bad and would have to come out. Kim's mother looked down at her sadly. "Kim," she said, "your throat will never be better until the tonsils come out."

Kim kept tugging and pleading, "But Mommy, I don't want an operation! I'm afraid!"

Her mother gave Kim a hug as they waited for the elevator. Two nurses were also waiting there. They understood why Kim was crying. They knew that nobody likes to have an operation, but sometimes people need them in order to get better.

Right after supper that evening, Kim went into the living room with her grandmother. Grandma lived with Kim and her mom. She always seemed calm and quiet and very wise. Grandma sat in the rocking chair embroidering a tablecloth. Tablecloths take lots of patience to make and Grandma had lots of patience.

"Grandma," Kim burst out, "I don't want an op-

21

eration!" She slipped down onto the carpet and hugged her favorite doll.

"I know, Kim," answered her grandmother. "I know how you feel. No one wants anything that hurts."

"Then why do I have to have an operation?" Kim whined.

"Because your throat will never get better until you have your tonsils out," Grandma answered softly. "You will always be sick. You want to be well and strong, don't you?"

"I still don't want an operation anyway," Kim pouted. "I don't want it!"

Grandma looked at Kim for a moment, and then began one of her stories about long ago.

"One night, Kim, when I was just your age, I was lying in bed crying big tears and trying to fall asleep."

"Why were you crying, Grandma?"

"Because I had a bad toothache," said Grandma. "My mother tried everything, but that toothache would just not go away. It filled every bit of me from the tip of my head to the bottom of my toes!"

"That must have been awful, Grandma," Kim said, shaking her head.

"It was, Kim, it was," Grandma nodded.

Grandma went on. "My mother rubbed some medicine on that tooth, saying, 'I know your tooth hurts, Agnes, but a hurt can be turned into good.' I didn't understand what my mother meant,"

Grandma admitted. "Then my mother said, 'Agnes, would you like to turn your hurt into a gift?'"

Kim wrinkled her nose. "How can you turn something that hurts into a gift?" she asked.

"By offering it to our Heavenly Father for love of him," Grandma answered. "That's what my own mother told me. She even taught me a little prayer: 'Dear God, I put up with this toothache for love of you.'"

"Did the toothache go away when you said that prayer, Grandma?" Kim asked hopefully.

"No, it didn't, Kim, but after I talked to God, I felt that he was very close to me, taking good care of me. I felt safe and brave and peaceful inside."

Kim hugged her doll. She looked up at her grandmother, and Grandma could see that Kim wanted to be brave, too.

"God wants us to take good care of ourselves and let the doctors help us when we are sick. We must try to be brave," Grandma explained. "We must try to offer our hurts to God, just like Jesus offered his hurt on the cross to God. That was the most beautiful gift anyone on earth ever gave. That gift helps us all go to heaven."

Kim wrapped her doll in a warm blanket and Grandma went on with her embroidering. Both were very quiet for a little while. Maybe they were talking to God about hurts....

The day came for Kim to go to the hospital and get ready for her operation. Kim kissed Grandma good-bye. She told her she was going to try to be brave, just like Grandma had been brave with her tooth-ache, and just like Jesus had been brave on the cross. Kim felt a little shaky inside, but deep down, she also felt strong.

Kim and her mother took the elevator they had taken before. They got off on the second floor where the two nurses worked. The nurses recognized Kim right away.

Kim and her mother stopped and asked the nurses where Kim should check in. The nurses could see that Kim's eyes were clear and bright. There was no tugging on her mother's coat, no crying.... Kim stood quietly waiting.

"What a brave little girl you are!" the nurse with the brown eyes said, taking Kim by the hand. She led Kim and her mother to the registration desk.

The first nurse came back and said to the other, "Now what do you think of that? Is this the same little girl we saw just a few days ago? She's really changed!"

But neither nurse could guess why, because neither one knew about the special talk that Kim had had with her Grandma. And neither one knew that Kim was being brave because she wanted to give her hurt to God. And even though this didn't take the hurt away, it made Kim strong and brave inside.

And now, I can tell you, Kim is all better and home from the hospital. She can talk and sing and yell and her throat is as good as new! But best of all, Kim turned her hurt into a beautiful gift for God. Now what could be better to do with a hurt than that?

Mean Until

Nighttime had come, and, as everyone knows, with nighttime comes bedtime. And the favorite part of bedtime for Tina, Scottie and Todd was always story time with their daddy!

Daddy would sit in his story-telling chair with Scottie and Todd tucked in their bed and little Tina on his lap. The lamp by Daddy's chair gave off a soft, warm glow—just right for a bedtime story.

"What's the story about tonight, Dad?" asked Todd, "Angels, heroes or spacemen?"

"Angels, angels!" squealed Scottie.

"Hold on, hold on!" laughed their dad. "There is an angel in our story tonight, but the story is really about a little boy. In fact, the story is called 'The Boy Who Was Mean Until...'

"Until what?" burst out Scottie.

"Shhhhh! Let Daddy talk," Tina insisted.

"Until...well that's the secret of our story," said Dad. "So let's begin!"

"Once there was a boy named Jeff. Now that doesn't sound like a mean name, does it?" Tina shook her head. Daddy continued, "Jeff lived with his mother and father, and little sister and baby brother. They all lived in a pretty green house right in the middle of the block. But everyone on the block used to say, 'That Jeffrey can sure act mean sometimes!' And, sorry to say, everyone on the block was right until..."

"Until what?" interrupted Scottie.

"Until Daddy says so," Tina added impatiently.

"Until one day, in the middle of the summer," continued Dad. "That day Jeff was feeling mean. Before lunch he bumped his little brother's foot with the back wheel of his bicycle. After lunch he pulled his sister's hair till she cried. Next he hit his friend Matt on the arm. Not once did Jeff stop to think about how his baby brother, his little sister

32

or his friend felt when he was mean to them. Not once did he think about how he had hurt them. And not once did Jeff think about saying he was sorry.

"That night, Jeffrey didn't even tell God he was sorry. When he remembered the mean things he had done that day he just laughed to himself and jumped into bed." Tina, Scottie and Todd all shook their heads. They knew that wasn't the right thing to do.

Their daddy continued with the story, "When Jeff was standing in front of the mirror combing his hair the next morning, he noticed two strange little bumps, one over each ear. They didn't hurt. They

only looked funny. Jeff went to show his mother. She had never seen that kind of bump before, so she gave Jeff breakfast and then called the doctor's office.

"'Hmmm,' the doctor said, 'one of my patients just canceled her appointment. Bring Jeff right over and I'll take a look.'

"The doctor carefully examined the bumps. He pressed them very gently here and there. He even took some X-rays, but everything looked fine. 'I really don't know what caused the bumps,' the doctor finally said, 'but there is certainly no danger. They will probably just go away on their own.'

35

"That night before falling asleep, Jeffrey thought to himself, *I wonder what these weird bumps are? I wonder where they came from?'* Suddenly he heard a kind voice answer, 'They're meanness bumps, Jeffrey.' Jeff opened his eyes and sat up. He was surprised to see his guardian angel standing by his bed."

Their daddy stopped for a minute and looked at little Tina. "Do you remember what a guardian angel does?" he asked.

"Yes, but tell us again, Daddy," Tina begged.

"God has given each one of us a special guardian angel. This angel watches over us and helps us live as God wants us to," Daddy explained. "Now back to our story," he said with a smile.

"'How did I get the meanness bumps?' Jeff asked his angel.

"'Only you know that answer, Jeff,' the angel said quietly. 'Do you want to talk about it?'

"Jeff nodded and the angel sat down beside him. 'If they're meanness bumps, I guess I got them from being mean,' Jeff said, looking down at his feet.

"'Has anyone ever been mean to you, Jeffrey?' the angel gently asked.

"'Uh-huh,' Jeff nodded.

"'Can you tell me about a time when someone was mean to you?'

"'Well, once when I struck out in an important Little League game some of the guys on my team wouldn't talk to me for a few days.'

"'And how did that make you feel, Jeff?' the angel asked.

"'Awful. Really awful and sad.'

"'How do you think your baby brother felt when you bumped his foot, or your sister when you pulled her hair, or your friend when you hit him?' the angel softly asked.

"'I guess they felt awful and sad too,' Jeffrey mumbled.

"'Would you like it if somebody did those things to you?'

"'No,' Jeff answered.

"'Jeff, Jesus taught us that we should love and be kind to other people. He said that we should always treat other people the way we want them to treat us. Do you remember learning about that?'

"Jeff nodded.

"'From now on,' the angel smiled, 'why don't you try doing what Jesus says instead of being mean?'

"'O.K.' Jeff answered in a squeaky voice, 'it sounds kind of hard, but I'll try.'

"'Don't worry, Jeff. If you ask God, he'll be very happy to help you,' the angel promised.

"After that Jeff couldn't see his guardian angel anymore. For a few minutes he sat there thinking about everything the angel had said. Then he whispered, 'God, I'm sorry for the mean things I've done. From now on I want to try to be kind and loving like your Son Jesus. Please help me. Amen.'

"The next day was Saturday and when Jeff got up, his bumps were still there. When he got to breakfast his mom had just finished feeding his baby brother. Jeff bent over the highchair and whispered in his brother's ear, 'I'm really sorry that I bumped into your foot yesterday.' His little brother squirmed and giggled. Jeff knew he couldn't understand the words, but that was O.K. Jeff felt warm and good inside after he said he was sorry. And...his meanness bumps started to get smaller.

After breakfast Jeff went out to play baseball with some of his friends. Just

as Doug was running to third base, Jeff's little sister Megan came by pushing her doll carriage. She got right in Doug's way and he made an out. All Jeff's friends got really mad and started yelling at Megan. She got scared and started to cry. At first Jeff felt like yelling at her too. Then he remembered what his angel had told him, 'Jesus asks you to treat others as you want them to treat you.' Jeff went over to his little sister and gave her a hug. 'It's O.K., Megan,' he said, 'I know you didn't do it on purpose. And you know what else? I'm really sorry I pulled your hair yesterday.' Megan stopped crying. Her little mouth curled into a big smile as she pushed her doll carriage back toward the house. And...Jeff's meanness bumps shrunk even more.

"Later that afternoon, Jeff decided to call his friend Matt. There was something important he needed to tell him. When Matt picked

up the phone Jeff said, 'Hi, Matt. It's Jeff. I missed you at the game this morning.'

"'I didn't think you wanted to play with me, after you hit me yesterday,' Matt said, sounding very sad.

"'Well, that's why I'm calling,' Jeff explained, 'I want to tell you I'm really sorry. Will you still be my friend?'

"'Sure!' Matt answered in a happy voice.

"When Jeff hung up he realized that something was different. He looked in the mirror and saw that his meanness bumps had completely disappeared! And that's the story of the boy who was mean until..."

"Until he learned to treat everybody as he wanted them to treat him!" Scottie broke in. Todd nodded and Daddy grinned. Tina was already fast asleep.

A Visit to Heaven

One night a little girl named Heather was saying her prayers. She added a special prayer that night for her friend, Chantal. Chantal had been very, very sick for a long time. Last week, Chantal had died. When Heather found out, she felt very scared and very sad. Then Heather and her mom and dad had a long talk. Heather's mom told her that heaven is a really special place where Chantal was living with God. "In heaven, there is no more sickness or sadness," Heather's dad had said. "It's a wonderful place of joy and love where God makes everybody happy." Even though Heather knew that Chantal was very, very happy with God in heaven, she still missed her a lot.

As soon as Heather had finished her prayers, she climbed into bed. On her window sill stood her miniature hot air balloon. It even had a basket for passengers to ride in, just like real balloons do. Chantal always had fun with the toy balloon whenever she had come over to

play. Just as Heather was dozing off to sleep, she thought she saw the balloon and basket start to grow! And then Heather had this beautiful dream....

The rainbow-colored balloon and its wicker basket continued to grow and grow and grow. Soon the balloon had squeezed itself right out Heather's window. It seemed to be waiting for Heather to wake up and go for a ride. When Heather did wake up (in her dream), you can imagine how surprised she was to see that her toy balloon had become real! Just as she was thinking, *I bet it could fly now*, she heard her guardian angel say, "Yes, it can and it wants to take you for a special ride, Heather. Climb right in. Don't be afraid!"

Heather quickly hopped into the balloon's big basket. She sat down on a seat with a spongy pink cushion. In a few seconds she was whooshing up, up, up into the sky. She couldn't see her house anymore.

Somewhere, and no one can tell where, the balloon floated through a cloud and softly landed a few steps away from a great golden door. *This must be a very special place, because this looks like a very special door*, Heather thought to herself. *I wonder where I am?*

Just then the great golden door opened. You can imagine how surprised Heather was when Chantal herself stepped through it! Heather had never seen Chantal look so beautiful and happy. Her eyes were shining with love and joy. Chantal gave Heather a great big hug. "I'm so glad to see you, Heather!" she cried.

Now Heather knew where she was! Beyond the golden door was heaven, the wonderful kingdom of God where Chantal now lived! As Heather watched in amazement, the golden door opened and closed once again.

"A new saint is arriving," Chantal explained.

"Chantal, what's it like inside?" Heather asked excitedly.

"Take three guesses," Chantal answered with a twinkle in her eyes.

Heather closed her eyes and thought hard. In a few seconds she guessed her first guess. "Is it like never ever having homework, or quizzes or tests?"

"No," Chantal giggled, "heaven is much better than that!"

With one guess worn out, Heather thought some more. "Is it like having a picnic at the beach with your best friends and your favorite food and music?"

"Oh no, Heather, heaven's much better than that!" laughed Chantal.

There was only one guess to go and Heather had saved her best guess for last. "Is it like having a birthday party with your mom and dad, brothers and sisters and all your friends, tons of presents and lots of ice cream and cake?"

"Heather, heaven is so much, much, much better than that!" grinned Chantal.

"Much, much, much better?" Heather gasped. "How can it be?"

"It's a zillion times better, Heather! It really is," Chantal answered with a beautiful smile. "You can't believe how happy we are here! We talk to God, we sing, we pray; here love's a light shining brighter than day. And since this is God's home, we're here to stay!"

As she said this, Chantal waved a happy good-bye and the golden door slowly closed. Heather was alone again, but she knew what to do.

She climbed back into the balloon's basket and soon she was whooshing through the clouds, heading straight for her window sill. In a few moments Heather saw the roof of her house. The next thing she knew the balloon had glided through her window and she was back in her bed.

When Heather woke up the next morning the very first thing she saw was her toy balloon. And now every time she looks at the balloon Heather remembers the wonderful dream of her visit to heaven. She especially remembers Chantal's happy words, "We talk to God, we sing, we pray; here love's a light shining brighter than day. And since this is God's home, we're here to stay!"

Grampy O'Shea Tells a Story

Jeremy and his little sister Tara followed a path through the thick bushes in back of their house. Jeremy held Tara's hand tightly as they ran across a field. It was the end of October and it looked as if someone had splashed bright red, brown and yellow paint on all the leaves and then rolled them thin with a giant rolling pin.

Jeremy and Tara were on their way to Grampy O'Shea's house. They always knew exactly where to find Grampy (the special name they gave their Grandpa) whenever they needed a good story. Today they found him fixing up his back porch.

"Oh! my favorite visitors are here!" Grampy greeted them with a grin. "It's good to see you two! It is. It is."

Even before Jeremy and Tara sat down on the porch steps, Tara squealed, "Grampy, aren't you going to tell us a story?" Jeremy and Tara knew that Grampy was as full of stories as he was of white hair, and that was a lot! Grampy's stories were different from

54

any that Jeremy
and Tara had ever
heard or read. They
left a warm feeling in-
side of you, kind of like
hot cocoa does on a cold
winter morning.

"Grampy, did you hear me?"
Tara asked loudly.

Grampy smiled and kept on
carefully painting the railing.
Then, sure enough, as Grampy
dipped his paintbrush into the paint
can again he began to tell a story with
a far-away sound in his voice.

22..

20...

16... 3

12...

10...

3...

2

1

"Across the wide ocean in the land where shamrocks grow, I once visited a monastery that was built on a high hill.

"If you counted all the monks who lived happily inside the monastery, you would have counted 72."

"That's a lot of monks, Grampy!" said Tara. She was thinking of how many times she would have to go around her fingers to count to 72.

Grampy nodded and smiled. "Some monks wrote books," he continued. "Some carved statues.

72!

70...

65...

53...

60...

45...

50...

48...

7...

34...

Some planted potatoes. Some grew beautiful flowers.

"But," and here Grampy's voice sounded quiet and mysterious, "there was one monk who didn't seem very talented. He couldn't write books. He couldn't carve statues. He couldn't even plant potatoes or grow beautiful flowers. And so he was given the simplest job of all. He answered the monastery door. His name was Brother Kevin."

Jeremy and Tara felt sorry for the monk who couldn't do anything special. They liked him right away.

"Now measured by books and skill," Grampy continued, "Brother Kevin was probably at the very bottom—he was number 72. But listen carefully now and see if you can guess the one thing in which Brother Kevin led all the rest!"

Jeremy and Tara sat up even straighter so they could listen better.

"It was one o'clock in the afternoon," Grampy O'Shea began again. "Cling-clang, cling-clang rang the monastery bell. All the monks headed toward their rooms to take a nap or to spend an hour of quiet time. They did this because they got up very, very early in the morning to pray.

"Brother Kevin headed for his room, too. He took off his sandals and was just about to rest his head upon the pillow when cling, cling, clang went the doorbell. Up sat Brother Kevin. He didn't frown. He didn't sigh. He didn't even grumble. He put on his sandals. Clip, clap, clippitty-clop down the quiet hall he went. He pulled open the big wooden door.

"'How can I serve you, Sir?' he politely asked the man who was standing there.

"'Brother Monk,' said the man, 'my children are hungry and we have no food.'

"'Please come in,' invited Brother Kevin with a big smile.

"The man stepped in. He sat on the bench near the door. He leaned his wooden cane against the wall.

"Straight to the kitchen went Brother Kevin. Soon he was back with a basket of food—cheese, three giant loaves of bread and some fruit.

"The man was so grateful. He smiled at Brother Kevin and said, "'Thank you, Brother! Thank you so much.' And down the steps he went carrying the basket.

"Back to his room went Brother Kevin. He sat on his bed and slipped off

his sandals. He was just about to rest his head upon the pillow, when cling, cling, clang sounded the doorbell.

"Up sat Brother Kevin. He didn't frown. He didn't sigh. He didn't even grumble. He put on his sandals. Clip, clap, clippitty-clop down the quiet hall he went. He pulled open the big wooden door.

"There was the same man, carrying the basket of food.

"'How can I serve you, Sir?' Brother Kevin asked politely.

"'Brother Monk, I forgot to tell you that I need some milk for the baby.'

"Off to the kitchen went Brother Kevin again. Soon he was back with a jug of cold, fresh milk in his hand.

61

"'Thank you, Brother, thank you so much!' the man said again. And he went down the steps with the basket of food and the jug of milk in his arms.

"Back to his room went Brother Kevin. He sat on his bed and slipped off his sandals. He was just about to rest his head upon the pillow, when cling, cling, clang sounded the doorbell.

"Up sat Brother Kevin. He didn't frown. He didn't sigh. He didn't even grumble. He put on his sandals. Clip, clap, clippitty-clop down the quiet hall he went. He pulled open the big wooden door. And who do you think was standing there?"

"That same man again?" Jeremy asked, shaking his head as if he couldn't believe it.

"Yes, that very same man," Grampy said with a grin.

"'How can I serve you, Sir?' Brother Kevin politely asked.

"'Brother Monk, I left my wooden cane the last time I was here.'

"Brother Kevin looked around. Sure enough, there was the wooden cane leaning against the wall.

"'Thank you, indeed, Brother!' said the man. 'Sorry to bother you!' Smiling and happy the man went down the steps with the basket of food, the jug of milk and his wooden cane.

"Back again to his room went Brother Kevin. He sat on his bed and slipped off his sandals. His head was just about to touch the pillow when cling-clang, cling-clang sounded the big monastery bell. It was two o'clock. The hour of quiet was over. It was time for all the monks to return to their work.

"Up sat Brother Kevin. He didn't frown. He didn't sigh. He didn't even grumble. Happily Brother Kevin clippitty-clopped his way to the bench by the door."

Grampy O'Shea put his paintbrush down and looked up at Jeremy and Tara. "Now maybe Brother Kevin was number 72

when it came to books and talents, but he was certainly number one in..."

"Patience!" cried Jeremy. Tara nodded.

"That's right," Grampy smiled, "Brother Kevin was the most patient of all the monks. And God was very happy about that."

By then it was time to go home. Grampy gave Jeremy and Tara each a hug. Then Jeremy took Tara by the hand and back through the field they went. As they climbed through the bushes behind their yard, Tara said, "You know what, Jeremy? Not everybody can be smart or know how to do special things, but everybody can be patient if they try."

"You know what, Tara?" Jeremy smiled, "I think you're right!"

The Blown-Around Room

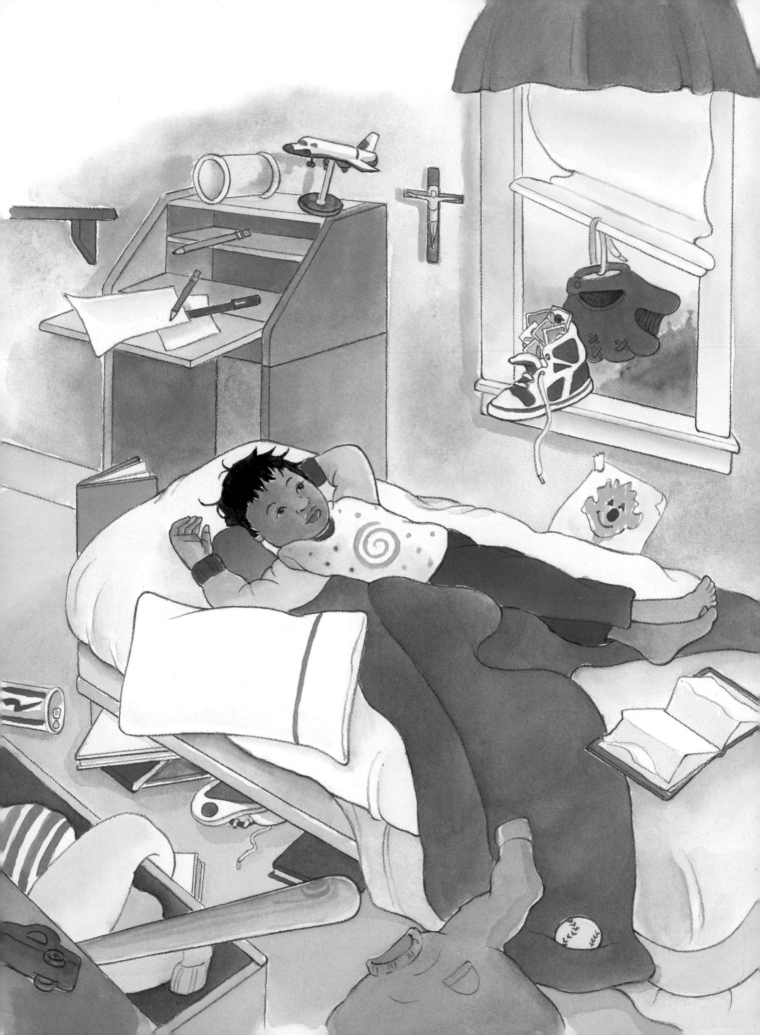

Anh (*Ine* as in "pine") had a very messy room. As a matter of fact, it looked like a big wind had come through the window and just blown everything around. Take a look at the picture and see for yourself. That's exactly what Anh's room looked like one Monday morning.

One sneaker was under the bed and upside down. The other one was sitting on the window sill—full of baseball cards! Anh's baseball bat was sticking out of the dresser drawer. His catcher's glove was tied to the window shade. His storybooks were scattered here and there and everywhere. His sweatshirt was crumpled up on the floor.

Yes, Anh's room looked like a big wind from the North Pole had just passed through. When his mother came in to call him for school that morning, she couldn't believe her eyes. "Anh, this is the most blown-around room I've ever seen!" she exclaimed.

Anh rolled out of bed. He started to kneel down to say his morning prayers. But first he had to move some videos, his bug collection and a few pairs of socks out of the way to make room. That was one thing about Anh, he might have a blown-around room, but he always said his prayers.

As Anh dumped the baseball cards out of his second sneaker, he could still hear his mom saying, "This is the most blown-around room I've ever seen!"

Would she be able to say that on Tuesday morning? Let's see....

When Anh got to the kitchen for breakfast, he saw something that made him happy. Spread out on the counter were celery, carrots, cabbage, eggs, ground pork, cooking oil, and thin, flat pieces of dough. Mom's biggest frying pan was sitting on the front burner of the stove.

Anh knew what all that meant—his mom was going to make something good! So Anh wasn't at all surprised when his mother announced, "Aunt Chung *(Choong)* is coming to visit and I'm going to make her favorite dish—egg rolls."

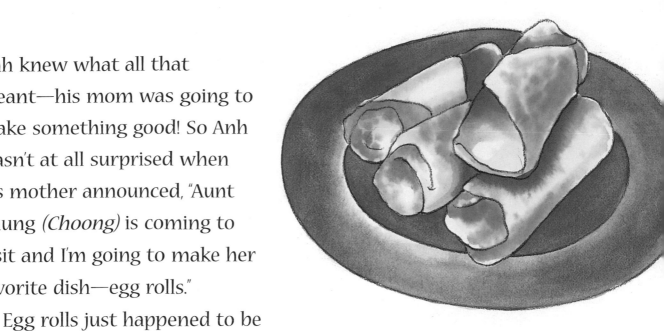

Egg rolls just happened to be Anh's favorite too! All the way to school Anh thought of the delicious meal he would find when he got home that afternoon. He could almost smell those egg rolls crackling in the frying pan. Aunt Chung would love the surprise! So would he!

But Anh's daydreaming didn't stop there. *Suppose, make believe, that someone was coming to visit me*, he thought. *Suppose, make believe, that that someone was Jesus! What special thing could I do for him?* All of a sudden Anh remembered his blown-around room. *If Jesus ever came to visit me, I know what I'd do*, he said to himself. *I'd clean my blown-around room for him!*

When Anh got home from school that afternoon, he went straight upstairs to his bedroom. He was thinking of his make-believe visit from Jesus. Anh closed the door. He looked around. His room really was very messy! He wasn't sure where to start, but he knew he had to start somewhere. First he picked up all his storybooks and lined them up in a neat row along the top of his desk. Then he put all the videos back into their cases and piled them on the empty shelf near his desk. Next he got a hanger and hung his sweatshirt in the closet. After that he untied his catcher's glove from the window shade, hooked it over his baseball bat and leaned the bat in the corner. Then Anh decided that it wasn't a very good idea to keep his bug collection on the floor. He might step on it someday. He carefully placed the cover on the box and slipped it into an empty drawer.

Finally Anh stood in the middle of the room. He turned first to the left and then to the right. Then he turned all the way around. His room didn't look blown-around anymore. Now he was ready for any visitor, even a very, very special visitor like Jesus!

That night after Anh had finished his prayers and was hopping into bed, he saw his guardian angel! The angel was smiling and holding a shiny silver mirror in his hand. Now this was a very special kind of mirror. It showed not just people and chairs and walls and lamps as all mirrors do. It showed what was in Anh's heart.

"Anh! Look into the mirror," his angel said. "What do you see?"

"I see Jesus!" Anh answered in a very surprised voice. "And I can tell by his eyes that he loves me very much!"

"That's right," the angel nodded with a smile.

Anh looked and looked at the mirror. He could have kept on looking forever, but all too soon the angel moved the mirror away. Then Anh could no longer see his angel.

Anh sat on the edge of his bed. He folded his arms across his heart and whispered, "Jesus, you didn't have to come visit me after all. Even though I can't see you, I know you are always with me, watching over me and loving me."

Anh made up his mind then and there that he would never let his room get blown-around again because each time he went into his room, Jesus went with him.

Anh slid off his slippers. He jumped into bed. He felt happy all over just thinking about how Jesus was living in his heart. Soon he was fast asleep.

On Tuesday morning Anh's mom came to wake him up. "Oh!" she said loudly as she looked around the room, "oh, I can't believe it!" Anh woke up, but he pretended he was still sleeping. He wanted to hear what else his mother would say. All the baseball trading cards were in a box. All the storybooks were standing on his desk. His sneakers were sitting side by side near his bed. The baseball glove and bat were leaning in the corner. The bug collection was hidden in the drawer. Did Anh hear his mom say, "Anh, this is the most blown-around room I've ever seen"? No! And he never heard her say it on Wednesday, or Thursday or Friday. In fact, he hasn't heard his mother say it till this very day!

Now Anh never forgets the wonderful truth that Jesus is always with him. And Anh wants to remind you that Jesus is always with you, too!

The Girl Who Was Afraid of the Dark

Jillian was afraid of the dark—so afraid that every night her mother had to sit by her bed till she fell asleep. Her mom even had to leave the bright bedroom lamp turned on all night long.

Jillian's mother tried to teach her to be brave in the dark. Each night at bedtime her mom reminded her, "Remember, Jillian, God is everywhere." Once she even asked Jillian, "Do you know where everywhere is?" just to make sure that Jillian did.

"Uh-huh," Jillian nodded, "everywhere is all over."

"So that means God is right here with you, Jill, even when you feel very scared," her mom explained. "God never ever leaves you alone."

A big wrinkle jumped onto Jillian's forehead. "But is God in the dark too, Mom?"

"He sure is. Even in the darkest dark!" her mother answered with a big smile. "And God can see just fine in the dark. He sees us and loves us and always watches over us—even in the darkest places."

Jillian knew that everything her mom said about God was true. It's just that it was hard for her to remember these things when she felt scared at night.

Now it happened that one dark and stormy night the light in Jillian's room burned out. There was a loud clap of thunder outside and Jillian woke up. Her room was dark, very dark. She couldn't see anything at all!

Jillian got very scared. She didn't want to be scared, but she just couldn't help it. In fact, you might say that Jillian was scared stiff, almost as stiff as a piece of cardboard. Jillian stayed scared and stiff in her bed all that night. She was still scared and still stiff the next morning. You can imagine how surprised her mother was when Jillian couldn't bend her knees to sit down at breakfast. She was just too stiff! So Jillian ate her breakfast leaning against the table. She had a little trouble picking up her toast and drinking her orange juice, too. After all, it's hard to move your fingers much when you're scared stiff.

That day Jillian felt too scared and too stiff to ride her bike or play basketball with her friends. When Jasmine and Nikki came to call her,

Nikki asked in surprise, "Jill, what happened? Why do you look so scared?" And Jasmine wanted to know, "Why are you so stiff, Jill?"

Of course, Jillian didn't want to tell her friends that she was scared stiff. So she let her mom do the talking. "Jillian didn't sleep well last night," her mom explained. "She'll be out to play again tomorrow."

Little by little, Jillian began to feel less scared and less stiff. That night, after she said her prayers, her mother tucked her into bed. "Now remember, Jill," her mom said as she pulled the soft blankets up to her chin, "God is right here with you, even in the dark. If you wake up and feel afraid, tell God you're scared. He understands and he'll help you. Will you try doing that, Jill?"

"O.K., Mom," Jillian whispered, "I'll try."

During the night Jillian slept soundly. But then, believe it or not, the lamp on her night stand went poof! and burned out. Once again Jillian's room was dark.

Jillian woke up. Her room was dark, very dark! She could have gotten very scared and even scared stiff all over again. But this time she didn't. This time she tried doing what her mother had told her. This time Jillian started to pray.

"Dear God, please help me not to be so scared. I know you are right here with me in this dark room. I know you are watching over me and loving me."

And do you know what? After talking to God, Jillian felt just a little less scared and not at all stiff. After a while, she even went back to sleep.

The next morning her mother walked into the room. Jillian was waiting for her with the covers pulled up to her chin.

The first thing her mother noticed was that the light was out. "Oh, oh!" she cried.

But that was as far as she got. In one great big leap Jillian jumped out of bed, threw her arms around her mother and hugged her tight.

"You were right, Mom! You were right! God is everywhere, even in the dark!"

Now Jillian's mother no longer sits by her bed until she goes to sleep. And instead of the bright bedroom lamp, only the night light stays on. Sometimes Jillian still feels scared in the dark, but when that happens, she knows what to do. She remembers that God is with her even in scary times, and she talks to him. And Jillian will tell you that talking to God can help to blow a scare far away.

And that's the best place for it, don't you think?

The Boy Who Thought God Was Hiding

Jason
was having breakfast.
In fact, half of his ce-
real was finished. His
mother took some toast
from the toaster and but-
tered it. "Did you say your
prayers this morning, Jason?"
she asked.

Jason put his head down so
his mom couldn't see his eyes.

"Guess I forgot again," he mumbled. He
twirled his spoon around in his cereal.
"Why can't I see God, Mom, just for a second? Then I
wouldn't forget him anymore."

Without waiting for his mother to answer, Jason
blurted out, "Is God hiding from me?"

"No, of course not!" his mom answered with a smile.

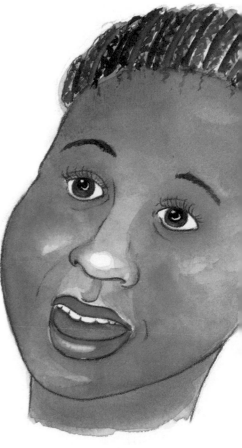

"You just have to learn how to look for him, that's all. Look carefully, Jason, and you'll find God. I promise."

Jason finished his cereal in a hurry. Where was he going to find God? He wondered.

Later that morning Jason's mother was in the basement washing clothes. Jason was in the family room playing with his model spaceship. All of a sudden, something that had never happened before happened. Jason saw his guardian angel.

89

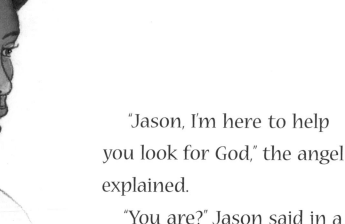

"Jason, I'm here to help you look for God," the angel explained.

"You are?" Jason said in a very surprised voice.

"Yes, I am," the angel answered in a very friendly voice. "Come with me. Don't worry. We'll be back before your mother misses you."

Without losing a moment, Jason was in his guardian angel's strong arms and they were sailing out the door and through the sky!

Jason lost count of the chimneys they passed, but soon they landed in the middle of a big pumpkin patch. Each orange pumpkin there looked big enough to make three pumpkin pies. Then the angel pulled out a large sheet of paper with golden letters on it.

Jason's eyes were wide with wonder. "What does it say?" he asked excitedly.

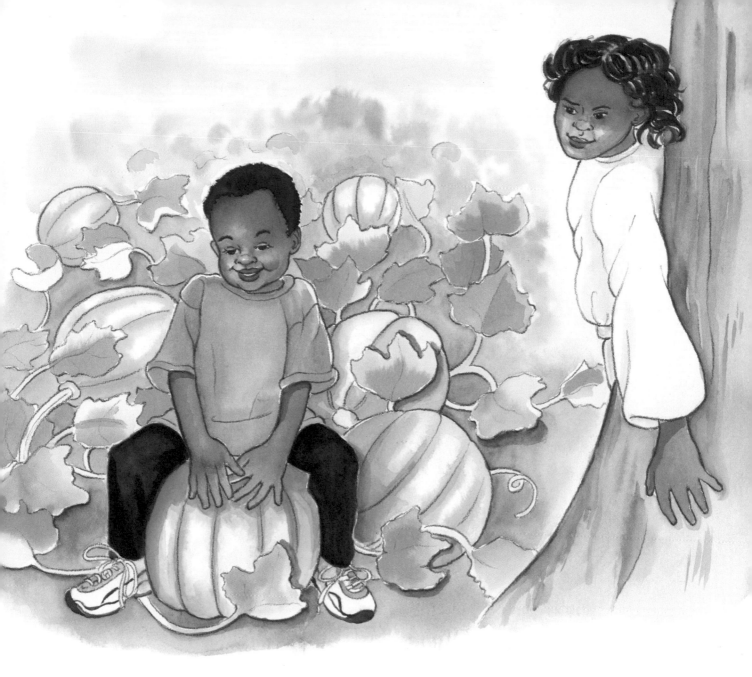

"It says, 'God is good, all good.'" the angel replied. The angel smiled at Jason and then pointed to the pumpkin patch. "Jason, these big pumpkins show you some of God's goodness. God makes the pumpkins grow and grow so you will have food to make you strong."

But the boy who thought God was hiding had nothing to say.

There was no time to waste because Jason and the angel had to be home before Jason's mom came up from the basement. So quick as a wink they were in the air again. Next they landed in a field of pretty white and yellow flowers—daisies to be exact.

Again his angel pulled out the large white sheet of paper with gold letters on it. "What does it say this time?" Jason quickly asked.

"It says, 'God is beautiful, all beautiful,'" answered the angel. The angel rolled up the paper and smiled down at Jason, who was as quiet as the shoelaces on his sneakers. "If you know how to look at flowers, they will show you some of God's beauty," the angel explained. "If you know how to look," the angel said again.

But the boy who thought God was hiding had nothing to say.

The angel once more scooped Jason up into his arms. This time they sailed over mighty ocean waves. As Jason watched, a great wave rolled and tossed a giant ship that weighed thousands of tons. Out came the white paper with the gold writing again.

"Read me the message," Jason begged the angel.

"God is mighty, all mighty," the angel read.

But the boy who thought God was hiding had nothing to say.

So the angel explained, "The ocean shows us some of God's power, Jason. That is, of course, if we know how to look."

94

Back over the
clouds went Jason
and his angel. On they
sped until they came to
some houses. Down below was a
little boy helping his sister up from a fall. Jason's angel
put him down in some cool, green grass. Out came the
white paper once more. "God is kind, all kind," read the
golden letters. This time the angel kept silent. He just
watched Jason very closely.

But the boy who thought God was hiding had nothing to say.

There was one last stop to make. Over a church they went. Somehow, the church's roof was as clear as glass and Jason could see inside. His angel pointed to a little girl who genuflected and went to pray by the tabernacle. Then the angel unrolled the white sheet and, sure enough there was a message for Jason on it. This time his guardian angel slowly bowed his head and, in a voice that was full of music, he softly read: "God is holy, so very holy." He bowed again and added, "All holy." Jason watched his angel who seemed to be praying.

But the boy who thought God was hiding had nothing to say.

The angel finally lifted his head and said, "Good people can show us some of God's holiness." He paused to smile at Jason, then he continued, "But we have to know how to look."

By then Jason's mother had almost finished the laundry, so the special trip had to come to an end.

Back through the door of Jason's house Jason and his angel sped. As the guardian angel set Jason down beside his model spaceship—where the wonderful trip began—he said, "Remember, Jason, you live in a world with a thousand mirrors. Everything God created is like a mirror that can help you to see God. The food you eat can show you God's goodness. Flowers can show you God's beauty. The ocean can show you God's power. People can show you God's holiness and kindness." And with those words Jason couldn't see his angel anymore.

Just then his mother came up from the basement.

"Mom!" Jason burst out, "do you know that we live in a world with a thousand mirrors?"

Jason's mother looked very confused. But Jason didn't even notice. He was too excited. He kept on talking. "We can see God in all the good things around us and in all the good deeds people do. Everything is like a mirror that shows us something about God!"

You can imagine that Jason's mother was very surprised. Was this the boy who had nothing to say? Was this the boy who was as quiet as his shoelaces? Was this the boy who thought God was hiding? Yes, it was! But now he had plenty to say about pumpkins and daisies and ocean waves and kind deeds and messages written in golden letters.

Never again did Jason ask, "Is God hiding?" And never again did Jason forget the secret way his guardian angel had taught him to look for and find God in the wonderful world around us!

Puff, Wrinkle and Squint

Our story begins in the home of a boy named Juan *(Wahn)*.

Juan had a four-year-old sister named Lupe *(Loop-ay)*. Now Juan was forever teasing Lupe—especially by making faces at her.

One Saturday morning, as Lupe was watching her favorite cartoon, Juan put on one of his mean faces. He puffed out his cheeks. He wrinkled his nose. He squinted his eyes. It was a mean sight for little Lupe to see over the TV set! But this time, Juan's mother caught him in the act. "Juan," she said, "if that face ever freezes, what will you do?"

Juan just laughed. He went right on teasing Lupe whenever his mother wasn't looking. He made more faces at Lupe during the commercials. He made some again before lunch. He even made mean faces during lunch.

It was during lunch that his mother noticed him again. "Juan, if that face ever freezes, you'll be sorry," she reminded him.

But Juan just laughed.

As soon as his mother turned her back, can you guess what he did? He put on one of his meanest faces. He puffed out his cheeks. He wrinkled his nose. He squinted his eyes. He was just getting ready to stick out his tongue when all of a sudden it happened...Juan's face froze tight! Now it was a rubbery kind of tight, but tight just the same. He couldn't get the puff out of his cheeks. He couldn't get the wrinkle out of his nose. He couldn't even get the squint out of his eyes. Puff, wrinkle and squint were there to stay!

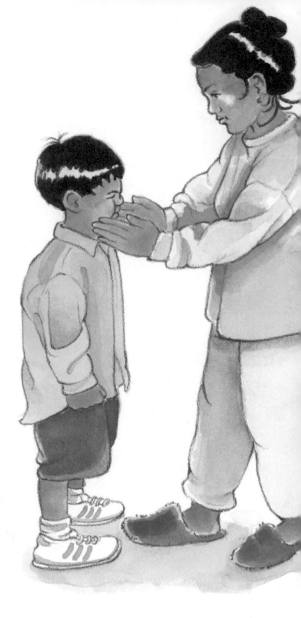

Juan showed his mother what had happened. But what could she do? She tried her best to press in his cheeks, but pop! out they puffed again. She stretched his nose to smooth out the wrinkle, but crinkle, crinkle! it wrinkled right up again. She rubbed Juan's eyes, but quick as a blink they squinted into a mean look again.

Yes, Juan's face was frozen. And that meant the mean look was there to stay.

Right after lunch Juan's friend David rang the doorbell. Juan's mother opened the door. "Juan can't come out and play today," she explained, "maybe tomorrow."

Juan watched from his bedroom window as David walked back to his yard. *This is no fun at all*, he thought. *Who would want to play with someone who has mean squinty eyes, a wrinkled nose and puffed out cheeks?*

Just then Juan's grandfather walked past the window. Juan always called him by the Spanish name for Grandpa, "Abuelito" *(Ah-bwel-ee-toe)*. Abuelito lived with Juan and his family. He loved taking care of the garden and making the yard look pretty. Juan knew his grandfather must be very smart because he had often heard his mother and father asking him questions.

Maybe Abuelito knows the secret for melting frozen faces, Juan suddenly thought. He pulled up the screen and leaned out the win-

dow. "Abuelito! Look what happened to my face! Can you help me straighten it out again?"

Abuelito looked up in surprise. After a minute or two he said, "If I were you, Juanito, I would try three things."

"You would?" answered Juan in a squeaky voice.

"Yes, I would," said Abuelito, nodding his head. "First I would think about what a mean face does to other people."

"It doesn't do anything, Abuelito. It's just a joke," Juan said.

"I don't know about that, Juanito," Abuelito answered as he scratched his head. "Do you think Jesus ever made mean faces at people?"

Juan had never thought about that. "No, I guess not," he had to say.

"I can tell you for sure that Jesus never made mean faces, Juan," Abuelito said. "Mean faces hurt other people. Jesus came to love us and to show us how to love one another. If you love someone, you don't want to hurt them, do you, Juan?"

"No," Juan answered quietly. For a few minutes he didn't say anything else. Then he asked, "If your face was

frozen in a mean look, what's the second thing you would try, Abuelito?"

"I would say I'm sorry to the people I made faces at. Then I would try to be very kind to them."

Juan thought about that for a few minutes as Abuelito stooped down and planted two pretty pink petunias right under Juan's window.

"And what's the third thing you would do?" Juan finally asked.

"I would tell Jesus all about the mean faces I made. I would tell him that I don't want to make them anymore. I would ask Jesus to fill my heart with more of his warm love."

"Thanks, Abuelito! Thanks a lot!" Juan called, pulling his head in from the window. He went over and plopped down on his bed. He had so much to think about!

After a little while, Juan started to talk to Jesus. "Dear Jesus," he prayed, "I'm really sorry for making faces at Lupe. I don't want to hurt her anymore. But now I have this bad habit of making mean faces. It's going to be hard to stop. Can you help me? Please send more of your warm love into my heart. Thank you, Jesus."

Juan felt good after he said this prayer. Somehow he knew that Jesus would help him.

Soon enough Juan jumped up and headed down the hall to Lupe's bedroom. The puff, wrinkle and squint went right along with him. Lupe was sitting on the floor making a puzzle. The picture on the puzzle box showed three little kittens curled up in a basket. At any other time Juan would have mixed up all the pieces just to tease his little sister. But not this time. This time Juan said, "Hey, Lupe, I'm sorry for making mean faces at you, O.K.?"

"O.K.," Lupe grinned. She looked back down at the puzzle pieces. Juan saw that she had only gotten a few of them to match. "It's hard," Lupe complained. "Wanna help?"

"O.K.," Juan agreed. He sat down beside Lupe

and helped her divide up the puzzle pieces.

First they looked for all the pieces that were part of the brown basket. Then they made a little pile of all the pieces of the golden kitten. Next they collected the pieces that would make the gray kitten. And then it happened! The puff in Juan's cheeks just puffed away!

Later that afternoon, Juan's dad asked if he would go upstairs and get a video Lupe wanted to watch. "Sure, Dad," Juan said.

As he bounded up the stairs, Juan felt a tingle in his nose. And before he knew it, the wrinkle there had stretched away! *Wow!* Juan thought as he rubbed his nose, *Whenever I let Jesus' warm love live in my heart I feel happy and close to him and my face even looks more like it used to!*

That night at supper there was ice cream and *pastel (pas-tehl)*, Juan's favorite kind of cake, for dessert. As his mother was getting ready to hand him his dish, Juan said, "Lupe first, Mom!" That did it! No sooner had Juan said these words than his squinty eyes opened wide and his mean look disappeared. The puff, wrinkle and squint were gone for good!

Never again did Juan give his little sister mean looks. And never again did Juan have any more trouble with the puff, wrinkle and squint. And if you ask him why, he'll tell you, "I want to be like Jesus.

Jesus knows that mean faces hurt other people. And now I know too. Jesus is helping me to be loving and kind and more like him, and that's just the way I want to be!"

Pattie Priscilla Pancake

The doctor tapped his fingers on his desk. "This is most unusual...most unusual!"

He had just tickled Pattie Priscilla under the chin with a feather. Any other girl or boy would have laughed and giggled. But not Pattie Priscilla Pancake. Pattie twitched one cheek and then the other, but try as she might, she couldn't laugh, she couldn't smile, she couldn't even giggle.

"Most unusual," the doctor mumbled again.

Other than not being able to laugh, or smile, or giggle, Pattie Priscilla could do lots of great things. She could fly kites, go roller-blading, blow up balloons, and eat lots of ice cream cones. But try as she might, she couldn't laugh, she couldn't smile, she couldn't even giggle.

While Pattie Priscilla was putting on her coat in another room, the doctor again tapped his fingers on his desk. "I'm afraid I don't have any medicine that can help her," he said.

Pattie's mother was worried. "But there must be something we can do, Doctor!" she exclaimed.

The doctor tapped his desk a little more. "Well, Mrs. Pancake, the only cure I can think of is for Pattie to see such a happy sight that she'll just have to laugh and smile and giggle." He nodded his head and tapped his desk and said again, "She'll just have to."

That night Mrs. Pancake told Auntie Til, her twin sister who was visiting, "Friday is Pattie Priscilla's birthday. Maybe a birthday party will be the happy sight that will make her laugh and smile and giggle."

"Maybe," said Auntie Til, who always agreed with her sister.

And so it happened that when Pattie came in from playing in the yard that Friday afternoon, all her friends were hiding in the dining room. "Happy Birthday, Pattie!" they yelled. "Surprise!"

Pattie could see Caitlin and Tommy and Brendan and Chelsea. She could see a pile of presents, a big bunch of balloons and a birthday cake that looked like a clown! It was indeed a happy sight for any boy or girl. But try as she might, Pattie Priscilla couldn't laugh, couldn't smile, couldn't even giggle.

It wasn't what the doctor had ordered....

"Oh, dear!" said Mrs. Pancake. "I'm so disappointed. I wonder what the happy sight could be?"

"Oh, dear! I wonder!" said Auntie Til, who always agreed with her sister. One week went by. Mrs. Pancake kept on thinking and wondering. "If only Pattie could laugh and smile and giggle," she sighed.

"If only she could!" repeated Auntie Til.

It wasn't too long, however, before the second happy sight was ready. One night, right after supper, Pattie Priscilla's mom made Pattie close her eyes really tight. Then she took her by the hand and led her into the playroom. "OK, Pattie! Open your eyes!" her mom cried.

There in the corner of the room stood the most beautiful doll house Pattie had ever seen! Every tiny room was filled with tiny furniture. Tiny curtains hung on the tiny windows. Even the tiny fireplace in the tiny living room had a tiny, make-believe fire in it! Pattie couldn't believe her eyes. She twitched one cheek, then twitched the other. She twitched and twitched but, try as she might, she couldn't laugh, she couldn't smile, she couldn't even giggle.

It wasn't what the doctor had ordered....

The following Sunday morning, after the family came home from church, Mrs. Pancake took Pattie Priscilla to the kitchen window. She pulled back the curtains and pointed. Pattie nearly jumped through the window with joy. There in the middle of the back yard stood a brown and white pony with a harness and saddle, all ready to ride. What a happy sight! Mrs. Pancake looked down at Pattie who twitched one cheek, then twitched the other. Pattie twitched and twitched but, try as she might, she couldn't laugh, she couldn't smile, she couldn't even giggle.

It wasn't what the doctor had ordered....

122

Mrs. Pancake sighed and said, "Pattie, why don't you go outside and play with your new pony? His name is Chuckles."

Dinner time came much too quickly for Pattie Priscilla. But as soon as her mother called her, she jumped right off her pony, tied his reins to the porch railing and hurried into the house.

Pattie Priscilla didn't know how to laugh or smile or even giggle, but she certainly knew how to obey.

That night, as Pattie was sitting on her bed taking off her slippers, she turned to see her guardian angel sitting right beside her.

"Pattie," her angel said in a very friendly voice, "I want you to see what a beautiful shine a good deed makes when it's seen from heaven."

Then the angel began to play something like a video right on the bedroom wall.

How surprised Pattie Priscilla was to see herself in the video! The video showed Mrs. Pancake calling Pattie in for dinner that Sunday. Next it showed her sliding off her new pony without a whimper or a frown. Finally the video showed how Pattie had obeyed her mom and come right into the house, even though she would have really liked to have kept on riding Chuckles.

Just at the point in the video when Pattie came into the house, she saw a beautiful bright light shining all around her. That was the shine made in heaven when Pattie Priscilla obeyed her mom!

It was such a happy sight that all of a sudden, without a single twitch, Pattie Priscilla began to laugh and smile and even giggle right out loud! Her angel smiled too. And then she couldn't see him anymore.

Such a happy sound was coming from Pattie's room that her mother dropped a potato chip in the living room. Auntie Til dropped another.

"Who could it be in Pattie's room?" Mrs. Pancake asked in surprise.

"Oh, who could it be?" repeated Auntie Til.

Mrs. Pancake and Auntie Til rushed to Pattie Priscilla's room. They opened wide the door. There on the side of the bed sat Pattie Priscilla, with one slipper on and one slipper off. She was just bursting with laughs and smiles and giggles.

"What happened?" asked Pattie's mother.

"What happened?" repeated Auntie Til.

Pattie told them the whole story and the next thing you know, Mrs. Pancake and Auntie Til were bursting with laughs and smiles and giggles too.

Pattie Priscilla Pancake (with a little help from her guardian angel) had found at last just what the doctor had ordered—the happiest sight of all—the beautiful shine a good act sends to heaven!

Christmas Looking

There it is—an old, skinny building at the end of the block. Can you picture it in your mind? Tyler lives there with his mother and father and his sister, Danielle.

They live on the fourth floor of that skinny, old building. Up the long flights of stairs we climb. Up to the door marked #44.

Now, of course, it wouldn't be very polite to just walk right in. But we're not really walking, we're just visiting in our thoughts, so let's open the door marked #44 and take a look.

There's not much to see inside. Just some plain furniture. But everything in the apartment is neat and clean.

"Tyler, we're leaving!" calls Mom. Mom and Danielle laugh to see Tyler come running. He bounces into the living room, pushing his arm through his jacket.

"You're always last, Tyler!" Danielle teases.

"Have a good time!" Dad calls from his bedroom.

It's the week before Christmas, and Tyler, Danielle and their mother are going Christmas *looking*. No, not Christmas shopping, just Christmas *looking*.

How do I know? Well, just listen to the children's mother: "Remember now, we're only going looking."

"No getting at all, Mommy?" ask Danielle and Tyler.

"No getting at all, not this time," Mom answers. "Maybe next Christmas," she adds with a smile.

Mom, Danielle and Tyler have their coats on now. And you can tell by looking at the coats that they're three, maybe even four

134

winters too old. That's because their dad has been sick for a long time. He hasn't been able to go to work and so the family doesn't have much money. But you don't need any money at all to go Christmas looking. All you need is a pair of good eyes. And God has given both Tyler and Danielle a very good pair of eyes!

Would you like to find out how their Christmas looking went?...

After they left the old, skinny apartment building Danielle and Tyler and their mom took a bus to a big shopping mall. Up the escala-

SANTA
Today →

tor at the mall Tyler and Danielle rode. Their mom couldn't keep up with them. "Wait for me!" she laughed. Now you don't need any money to ride an escalator. Just a pair of strong legs. And God had blessed Tyler and Danielle with strong legs.

Toyland was on the third floor. What a ride! If Tyler looked down as the escalator was going up, he could see the Christmas decorations upside down! "Danielle, look back!" he yelled. "I can't...it makes me dizzy!" Danielle giggled.

As they stepped off the escalator, a wonderful smell filled the air. Danielle sniffed and sniffed, wiggling her nose like a bunny rabbit. "Ooooo...Christmas trees!" she squealed. Sure enough, Toyland was full of real live Christmas trees decorated from top to bottom in spar-kling lights. In the middle of Toyland sat Santa Claus himself. His head was bent as he listened very closely to what every girl and boy was asking for...a doll or a video, sometimes even a computer game or a new bike.

"Can I tell Santa something, Mom?" asked Danielle. Her mom looked a little worried, but just for a minute. "Of course, honey," Mom smiled. "Go right ahead."

Danielle waited her turn and then climbed up on Santa's knee. "Santa, my name is Danielle. We can't get any toys this year, but can you still make it the best Christmas for my family?"

Santa looked straight into Danielle's green eyes and gave her his most special smile. "I promise that if you look for the secret of Christmas you'll find it, Danielle, and this *will* be the best Christmas ever." As he helped Danielle slide off his knee, Santa said, "Look for the secret, now. So many boys and girls miss it...they only think about getting toys. Good-bye, Danielle! See you next year."

And where was Tyler all this time? He had found the electric trains. Through the tunnels and toy cities they buzzed, across a river, up the hills, zigzagging around a mountain then back down to the station.

Tyler watched and watched. "Thank you God for the gift of my eyes," he whispered. "It's a lot of fun to just watch the trains."

Tyler would probably still be there if his mother hadn't called him, "Tyler! Danielle wants to hear the music boxes. Let's go!"

Danielle and Tyler and their mom must have listened to every happy song in every pretty music box at the counter. But all the time a big question kept popping into Danielle's head. *What's the secret of Christmas?* Danielle didn't know. Maybe it had something to do with gifts. *Being able to hear this pretty music is a gift*, she thought to herself. *So is having a good time.* "Thank you, God, for these gifts," Danielle said in her heart.

After discovering all there was to discover in Toyland—and that was a lot—Danielle and Tyler and their mom decided to ride all the way up on the escalator then all the way down again—just for fun. When they finally reached the bottom, it was almost time to go home.

It was *then* that the Christmas lookers found the very best thing in the mall.

Can you guess what it was? There in the aisle near the movies was a little shop that sold Christmas manger scenes from all over the world. There were Nativity scenes from Italy, Germany, Switzerland, France and Holland...just too many to count.

Tyler ran ahead. Danielle and Mom followed him into the store. Every shelf was neatly arranged with statues big

and small. Baby Jesus, Mary, Joseph, angels, shepherds, sheep, donkeys, cows, the three kings and the camels were all there. There were even wooden stables of all shapes and sizes. Danielle and Tyler knew why. Their mom had told them the Christmas story many times.

Danielle pointed to a statue of Baby Jesus with real glass eyes. "Look, Tyler," she announced, "Baby Jesus didn't have fancy clothes either. No matter what country he comes from, he's always poor!"

Tyler nodded. Then their mom bent down like she always does when she wants to say something important. "Jesus loves us more than anyone else has ever loved us. He loves us more than anyone else will ever love us," Mom said. "Jesus' love is his best gift to us. It's also the best gift we can give one another. Love is the secret of Christmas!"

Even though they were going home without any new toys or gifts, Danielle and Tyler suddenly felt very warm and happy inside.

It was almost time for supper by then. The three Christmas lookers took a bus back to the old, skinny building at the end of the block. Up the long flights of stairs they climbed. All the way up to the door marked #44. Dad was sitting on the couch waiting for them. He wanted to hear all about their adventures.

Danielle and Tyler were very sleepy and very happy when they knelt down to say their prayers that night. Going Christmas looking had reminded them of how many wonderful gifts they already had. Tyler and Danielle had special gifts that all the money in the world can't buy because these gifts come from God. You have these gifts too. You can walk, you can see, you can talk, you can hear and touch and smell and—best of all—you can love. And, as everybody knows, these gifts are worth more than all the toys in Toyland put together!

Narrow Henrietta

She
didn't live in a nar-
row house. Nor did
she have a narrow
mother or father.
She didn't eat a nar-
row dinner. And she
certainly didn't have a
narrow name. That's
why it is so surprising
that she became a nar-
row girl. Yet, when you hear
how it happened, it isn't so surprising after all.
Her name was Henrietta Hempstead and she was born
healthy and round, round, that is, as any baby should be. It
seemed certain that she would always be healthy and round,
but then something happened, sad to say. As Henrietta
turned four, then five, then seven, then eight, she thought
more and more of herself and less and less of her mother
and father, her three sisters and her friends. Henrietta hardly
ever talked about anything or anybody but herself!

One night, after Henrietta and her three sisters had gone to bed, her mother was talking to her father. "I'm worried about Henrietta," Mrs. Hempstead said. "Have you noticed how she only thinks about herself?"

"Yes," answered Mr. Hempstead. "She worries me too."

"This morning," continued Mrs. Hempstead, "when Lisa was telling us about how she lost her snack money on the way to school, Henrietta just shrugged her shoulders and said 'That's no money out of my piggy bank!'"

Mr. Hempstead shook his head. "And just before supper," he said, "when little Beth fell off her bike and scraped her face, all Henrietta said was, 'That's no skin off my nose!'"

Yes, Mr. and Mrs. Hempstead were very sad about the way Henrietta was acting.

Meanwhile, Henrietta had just fallen asleep. As she was sleeping, there came a sound of pinching and shrinking from under her blankets. Believe it or not, Henrietta was shrinking. She began to squeeze together and get narrow! The shrinking and squeezing went on all night. When Henrietta got up the next morning she found that she was as narrow as a toothpick! And so the girl who always thought only about herself had become as narrow as her thoughts.

You can imagine how surprised her mother was when she saw Henrietta at breakfast. But Mrs. Hempstead tried to be brave. She fixed Henrietta a big

152

bowl of puffed rice cereal hoping that it would puff her back to normal. She poured on cream and sugar. She toasted bread and spread it thickly with jam. But even after eating such a wonderful breakfast, Henrietta was as narrow as before. Her mother couldn't get her rounded out again.

At the school bus stop that morning, the bus drove away before Henrietta could get on. Henrietta was so narrow that the bus driver didn't see her!

That night, when the whole family was watching TV in the living room, her sister Kathy sat right on Henrietta's lap. Kathy jumped up and apologized, "I'm sorry, Henrietta, but I didn't see you sitting there!"

Big tears filled Henrietta's eyes. Henrietta knew why she had become narrow. She had often heard her dad say, "Selfish people get so
narrow inside." And Henrietta had been selfish. She leaned closer to
her dad who was sitting beside her on the couch. "Dad, how can I get
round again?" she asked as a tear trickled down her cheek. Mr.
Hempstead put his arm around her shoulder. "I know a special kind of

medicine that's sure to make you round again, Henrietta. Jesus told us about this medicine a long time ago."

"What's the medicine?" Henrietta asked excitedly.

"Thinking of others and loving them," her dad answered. "Jesus taught us to do this when he said, 'Love one another as I have loved you.'"

Henrietta went to bed that night thinking about what her dad had told her. Then she thought a lot about Jesus and his love for other people. Finally she started thinking about how she could help her mother and father around the house and be kind to her sisters and friends. These were brand new thoughts for the little girl who used to think only of herself.

A wonderful thing happened that night. Tiny popping, puffing out and stretching sounds came from under Henrietta's blankets. Little by little Henrietta began to stretch and widen and get round again! The thoughts of others found the space inside Henrietta too cramped and small and tight and they pushed and tugged away till the space got big and wide and open. In the morning Henrietta was all round again!

Henrietta's dad couldn't believe his ears when she announced, "Next week is Mommy's birthday, and I have just enough money in my piggy bank to get her a present." This was a new Henrietta, all right, a Henrietta who was thinking about others.

Now Henrietta keeps on thinking of others and loving them because she knows that this is what makes her beautiful and bright like Jesus on the inside. Being round on the outside is important, but Henrietta will tell you that being bright and beautiful and open like Jesus on the inside is what counts most of all. Don't you agree?

Pauline
BOOKS & MEDIA

The Daughters of St. Paul operate book and media centers at the following addresses. Visit, call or write the one nearest you today, or find us on the World Wide Web, www.pauline.org.

CALIFORNIA
3908 Sepulveda Blvd., Culver City, CA 90230; 310-397-8676
5945 Balboa Ave., San Diego, CA 92111; 858-565-9181
46 Geary Street, San Francisco, CA 94108; 415-781-5180

FLORIDA
145 S.W. 107th Ave., Miami, FL 33174; 305-559-6715

HAWAII
1143 Bishop Street, Honolulu, HI 96813; 808-521-2731
Neighbor Islands call: 800-259-8463

ILLINOIS
172 North Michigan Ave., Chicago, IL 60601; 312-346-4228

LOUISIANA
4403 Veterans Memorial Blvd., Metairie, LA 70006; 504-887-7631

MASSACHUSETTS
Rte. 1, 885 Providence Hwy., Dedham, MA 02026; 781-326-5385

MISSOURI
9804 Watson Rd., St. Louis, MO 63126; 314-965-3512

NEW JERSEY
561 U.S . Route 1, Wick Plaza, Edison, NJ 08817; 732-572-1200

NEW YORK
150 East 52nd Street, New York, NY 10022; 212-754-1110
78 Fort Place, Staten Island, NY 10301; 718-447-5071

OHIO
2105 Ontario Street (at Prospect Ave.), Cleveland, OH 44115; 216-621-9427

PENNSYLVANIA
9171-A Roosevelt Blvd., Philadelphia, PA 19114; 215-676-9494

SOUTH CAROLINA
243 King Street, Charleston, SC 29401; 843-577-0175

TENNESSEE
4811 Poplar Ave., Memphis, TN 38117; 901-761-2987

TEXAS
114 Main Plaza, San Antonio, TX 78205; 210-224-8101

VIRGINIA
1025 King Street, Alexandria, VA 22314; 703-549-3806

CANADA
3022 Dufferin Street, Toronto, Ontario, Canada M6B 3T5; 416-781-9131
1155 Yonge Street, Toronto, Ontario, Canada M4T 1W2; 416-934-3440

¡También somos su fuente para libros, videos y música en Español!